THE TROJAN HORSE

RETOLD AND ILLUSTRATED BY
WARWICK HUTTON

MARGARET K. MCELDERRY BOOKS
New York

MAXWELL MACMILLAN CANADA
Toronto

MAXWELL MACMILLAN INTERNATIONAL
New York • Oxford • Singapore • Sydney

— for Zander —

Margaret K. McElderry Books
Macmillan Publishing Company
866 Third Avenue
New York, NY 10022

Maxwell Macmillan Canada, Inc.
1200 Eglinton Avenue East
Suite 200
Don Mills, Ontario M3C 3N1

Macmillan Publishing Company is part of the
Maxwell Communication
Group of Companies.
Printed in China
10 9 8 7 6 5 4 3 2
The text of this book is set in Palatino.
The illustrations are rendered in watercolor and pen on paper.

Library of Congress Cataloging-in-Publication Data
Hutton, Warwick.
The Trojan horse / retold and illustrated by Warwick Hutton. — 1st ed.
p.   cm.
Summary: A retelling of how the Greeks used a wooden horse to win
the ten-year-long Trojan War.
ISBN 0-689-50542-6
[1.—Trojan War. 2. Mythology, Greek.]   I. Homer. Iliad.   II. Title.
BL793.T7H87 1992   91-21590
398.2′0938—dc20

Many thousands of years ago, the Greeks and the Trojans were at war. Paris, the son of King Priam of Troy, had fallen in love with Helen. But Helen was already the wife of Menelaus, who was the king of Sparta, a Greek city. When the lovers fled to Troy, the furious Menelaus gathered a huge army of Greeks and sailed after his wife.

The Greeks camped before the gates of Troy, where the Trojans could look down at them from the city ramparts. Many battles were fought—and there were many brave heroes—but the armies were equally matched. For weeks, for months, for years, both sides fought, watched, waited, then fought again. Camp fires flickered, guards shouted orders, horses neighed. But no side won.

Then one morning, ten years after they had arrived, the Greek army began to leave. Clouds of dust rose up. The camp echoed with shouted orders and the noisy clatter of men dismantling tents and mounting horses. The Greek soldiers, shields and swords shining in the morning sun, moved down to the shore and into the waiting ships.

From the walls of Troy the Trojans watched. As the Greek ships sailed away, the Trojans came cautiously out of the city gates. The enemy had gone, but as the clouds of dust settled over the campground, a huge shape appeared.

There, standing alone, was an enormous horse made of wood. It had painted eyes and a bright face. The Trojans walked around it carefully. At last, Laocoön, the high priest of Troy, came out. "Never trust the Greeks," he said. "There must be some trickery in this horse."

He looked at its great round belly. Then he took a spear from a guard standing beside him and flung it at the horse's side. The spear quivered as it struck and there was a strange hollow echo. But the Trojans were in no mood to listen to Laocoön's warning, so, with his two young sons, he departed to make a sacrifice.

Meanwhile, at the water's edge, the Trojans had found a small man whose hands were bound behind him. He looked imploringly at them.

"Let's kill him. He's a Greek," some said.

"Oh, let him go. If the Greeks have tied him up, he's probably on our side," said others. As they began to untie him, they questioned him:

"What's your name?"

"What happened to you?"

"Can you tell us what this great horse is for?"

The man started to talk. "My name is Sinon. The others were going to kill me because the high priests said that to win the war they must build this great horse as a gift for the

goddess Athena and make a human sacrifice. I was to be the sacrifice. They bound me hand and foot, but I managed to free my legs and escaped and hid."

The Trojans looked at each other in puzzlement as Sinon continued.

"Their one great fear is that you will drag the horse into your city. Then all the goddess Athena's favor and protection will go to you instead of them, and they will never be able to win the war. To prevent this, they have carefully made the horse too big and heavy to fit between the city gates."

The Trojans listened carefully. Some did not believe Sinon, but then, as if to persuade them, an extraordinary event occurred.

From the direction in which the Greek ships had gone, two enormous sea snakes appeared. They glided through the calm blue water toward Troy. As the people watched in fearful fascination, the snakes slithered from the surf, up the shore, past the wooden horse, and on to where Laocoön and his sons were sacrificing a bull. With terrible ferocity the snakes struck. Twisting their bodies first around the sons, and then the father, they killed all three. The Trojans looked on in horror.

"It must be a sign. The gods have punished Laocoön for doubting the wooden horse," they said, and then: "Let us widen the city gates and pull it through."

"Get tree trunks. We'll move the horse with rollers."

With ropes and rollers they started to move the horse. As they pulled, some said they could hear a curious metallic echo that seemed to come from inside the huge wooden body. But the singing and shouting of happy Trojans soon drowned out all other sounds, and the wooden horse moved forward.

At last, after the city gates had been widened, the great wooden horse stood in the central square of Troy. It seemed to smile down at the people as they danced around it and sang of their new freedom.

Evening came and then the night. Exhausted by the day's excitement and triumph, the Trojans went to their beds and fell into a deep and peaceful sleep.

That night there was no moon. Inky darkness covered Troy. It covered the seashore outside the city walls, and out to sea there was a deeper blackness. The painted eyes of the wooden horse stared at the night. On the city ramparts, Sinon was watching through the darkness, looking out to sea. Suddenly there was a golden flicker of fire, a signal from a ship. Sinon stood up. He had been waiting for that signal. The Greek ships had returned. Quickly and quietly he moved down and across the square to where the horse was standing.

Inside the horse, it was hot and dark. Instead of being solid wood, the great body was hollow—and it was filled with armed men. Armor, swords, and helmets gleamed in the weak light of one tiny lamp.

On the outside, Sinon put up a ladder, climbed to the side of the belly, and opened a trapdoor. A host of armed soldiers poured out. Their swords and shields clanged in the dark, but they moved quickly. Soon the sleeping guards were captured. The city gates already lay open—destroyed to bring in the horse.

In the darkness the Greek army had landed again on the shore, and now a horde of soldiers entered into the city.

That night, ten years of waiting were over. Greek soldiers swarmed through Troy, burning, breaking, and destroying the city.

People ran everywhere in confusion, trying to find their friends and belongings. The Greeks gathered rich plunder, and by morning the Trojans who were still alive left their broken city in a weeping trail of conquered people.

Everyone had forgotten Paris and Helen, who had started it all. But there in the city square stood the wooden horse, and over the smoking ruins of Troy its bright painted eyes still gazed.